Call

To

PURPOSE

A novella of repentance, deliverance, hope and salvation

By Marni M. Williams

Williams Enterprise Productions
Producing From the Depth of the Spirit
A Conceptualization of Creativity

ISBN 0-9727687-1-8
Library of Congress Control Number: 2003093820

Published in the United States by:
Williams Enterprise Productions
c/o Marni M. Williams
P.O. Box 812
Middletown, Delaware 19709
Phone: (302) 376-4379
e-mail: Williamsenterpriseproductions@msn.com &
        Marniwilliams@msn.com

www.marniwilliams.com
Additional copies of this book are available online or by mail.

TO GOD BE THE GLORY

Cover Photography Copyright © 1997 by Morris Press

Printed in the United States by Morris Publishing
3212 East Highway 30 • Kearney, NE 68847 • 1-800-650-7888

Acknowledgements

I give all glory, honor and praise to God and give thanks to Him for blessing me and calling me according to His perfect purpose and will through our Lord and Savior, Jesus Christ. It is only by the grace and mercy of God, that I can do anything at all. To my awesome husband, Mark, thank you, for showering me with unconditional love, support and encouragement. I am extremely blessed to be able to share my life, dreams and love with such an intelligent, caring and loving human being (not to mention, handsome). God's timing and plans are perfect. I love you dearly.

To my loving, supportive family: mom, Heidi, grandmom and all of my family, thank you for being there. I love you. Mom and grandmom, thank you for the example of faith, perseverance, determination and courage. Heidi, I thank God that He made us spiritually connected, brought forth through the same vessel (awesome plan). You've been with me for a lifetime and eternity (big sis).

I am grateful for a very special group of people, without whom, this book would not have been birthed: The Faith Based Literary Extravaganza Family. Thanks Audrey Williams, Victoria Christopher Murray, Patricia Haley, Maurice Gray, Jacquelin Thomas, Terrance Johnson and James Guitard. Omah, thank God you were obedient to the voice and vision of God. You are such a blessing. Victoria, thank you for caring, sharing,

iii

loving, mentoring and editing (and thank you for sharing that poem I love so much). Patricia, thank you for sharing your vision, wisdom, humor and expertise (editing and business) with me. Maurice, thanks for putting a sister down with resources, information, editorial assistance and a listening ear. Terrance, thank you so much for your encouragement and Jacquelin, thank you for your prayers. James, your role was instrumental in my call in a new direction. Peace and blessings, my brother. I thank God for placing all of you in my life to assist in my call to purpose.

Thank you, Carlette, for your support, encouragement and for the gift of love, sharing and caring. Thanks Doreen for your words of confirmation. God is good. Christine and David, thank you for over 10 years of a wonderful friendship and for 10 years of an example of Godly family values and wisdom. I couldn't ask for better neighbors. Mr. & Mrs. Boswell, thank you for your undying support and encouragement. Thank you, Mrs. Boswell for pushing me towards my first leadership experience in college. You were an angel sent by God to greet me at the door. Hallelujah. Ms. Wilbon, if I didn't know any better, I'd think you were Mrs. Boswell's sister angel. Your role was very similar. Thank you for the support and encouragement. Your faith in my abilities helped lay the foundation for law school.

To Impact Deliverance Center, God used you with words of confirmation. Deliverance, power and authority are mine.

Dedication

This book is first dedicated to God and then to my loving and supportive soul-mate, best friend and husband, Mark and to my four beautiful children, Johnathan, Jonai, Myah and Egypt. I love you all.

Foreword

We are born with the innate ability from God to accomplish the purpose that He has ordained for our lives. Every part of our personalities, hopes, dreams and passions are directly related to that purpose. Isn't this awesome and exciting? This journey begins with careful examination of the things that we love to do, submission to the voice that speaks from within, and faith in God and His creation of redemption, salvation and righteousness for us, the Messiah, Jesus.

After spending my time and money on seven years of school (four years of college and three years of law school) and five years practicing law, I have finally stepped into God's purpose for my life. This is a beautiful place! His plan was so awesome that I could have never fathomed this outcome or planned it better.

Through trials, tribulation and doubt, He has been faithful and true to accomplish the purpose that He has called me to, so that He can get the glory and honor. Like Gideon in the Bible (Judges 6-8), I asked for confirmation, time and time again. And time after time, He was faithful to provide that confirmation. He meticulously placed experiences and people in my life to get me to this point.

If this story reminds you of the story of Gideon, that is no coincidence. Although it is not intended to be the exact story as rendered in the Bible, it is fashioned, in a contemporary sense, after the story of Gideon.

I decided to translate the war that Gideon fought to the modern day war against the mindset of the African-American people and, in particular, the African-American male population. This battle includes the war against drugs and violence in the African-American community. My heart bleeds for all of the brothers out there, killing each other and incarcerated. My heart aches for the children who are being raised without their fathers. May God have mercy on us all.

I pray that this story inspires you to seek God's divine purpose for your life.

To God be the glory!

I do what I do best

When He pushes me out of the nest

In search of His will

And until…

I'll find no rest

Life alone will be the test

I flap my wings

I almost fall

Weak and frail

I am young and small

He blows His breath

Here comes the wind

It lifts me up high

My time to spend

My wretched soul in search of the way

Storms rain by with life's trials

Here I sway

But He helps me on course

He guides me to His way

I cherish this day

Oh hear me say

I cherish this day!

~One~

In the breeze of the pitch black night, his heart vigorously thumped on the wall of his chest like the pounding of his feet on the concrete and the panting of his breath. Fast. Hard. Steady. His head turned about frantically and his eyes darted in every possible direction looking for another place to run. Panic mercilessly choked his heart as adrenaline surged fear throughout his psyche. The deal had gone bad, and his theft of the goods had been discovered. The chase that lasted over five minutes and started with his cohort running along side of him seemed to have come to a sudden halt. The neighborhood he lived in for the seventeen years of his life afforded him no escape route; he was walled in with nowhere to run. His pace reluctantly slowed as his body jerked around and his arms flailed while he looked for options that didn't exist. It was over. The representative of the west side gang honed in on his prey. Bang!

The sound was deafening to his ears and the pain that followed, almost within an instant was deafening to his soul. The fiery heat stung and seared his flesh forcing him to slump on his knees. Just like that, he was gone, not having processed the shot to the head or the first bullet's final destination to his heart.

~

His mother's wailing cries could be heard throughout the neighborhood and the heavens. "Ohhhh God. Pleeeeeasse Lord. Have mercy on this generation of the lost. Have mercy on us."

~

Gilman spread the damp shirt neatly on the back of the chair so that it hung evenly on both sides. He reached into the clothes basket for the pair of pants on the top and searched around the room for a door or another chair that he hadn't used. He flung the pants in the air to press out the wrinkles, opened the closet and threw them over the top of the door. He listened carefully as the words of the preacher on the radio caught his attention. "We must embrace truth, move to repentance and serve God and only Him. We must put away every work of idolatry, which is anything that you put before God: your job, your spouse, your children, material possessions, music,

2

television, food. Where are your thoughts, time and money spent? If they are not serving God and His purpose for your life, you should repent."

Suddenly, he heard a voice emanating from the doorway. *"God is with you, strong warrior, defender of your people."*

He whirled around in shock and amazement, almost loosing his footing as he turned. No one was there!

After peering at the doorway for a few seconds, he slowly turned to return to his task. He spoke with a sarcastic tone in response to what he thought was just his imagination. "Strong warrior! Me? Look at me - hanging clothes around the house instead of outside on the clothesline to keep from ducking and diving bullets or avoiding the crack head's shopping spree. And if God is with me and my people, why do we suffer so, as if He has abandoned us?"

"Take heart. God is with you in your journey."

He shook his head and stared at the doorway one more time.

"Oookay. I must really need some rest. I'm going to sleep good tonight," he said to himself as he continued to hang clothes.

~

The tumultuous turning of his stomach forced his eyes open and his body awake. Gilman sat up in the twin bed that he had slept in for the past 15 years and rubbed his eyes. He squinted at the clock. Three o'clock. His stomach continued to bubble as he hurriedly made his way to the bathroom. He thought back to the meals he had eaten. He was lactose intolerant but nothing in his stomach warranted a sudden trip to the bathroom in the middle of the night.

As he sat there relieving his ailing bowels, he stared into space with his mind wandering. As if having a daydream, he saw himself standing on the corner of his neighborhood called Riverside; Wilmington, Delaware to be exact. The projects. He was still fairly young, wearing a pair of jeans, a cream turtle neck shirt and a black leather jacket. He saw himself standing on the corner, with several young people standing around him.

He heard himself speak. "You don't have to stay where you are. You don't think because you've been taught not to think. This is what you've accepted. There's another existence out there waiting for you to discover and live. If you accept what you've been told, without reading and discovering for yourselves, how will you know? Jesus came to set you free and only God can make you whole again. I was born here, just like you. No one in my family graduated from high school, let alone

4

college. Yet I stand here before you with a semester of college under my belt, only by the grace and mercy of God. You too can have freedom and salvation by accepting Jesus as the Messiah, sent by God as the sacrifice for your sins and the only way to righteousness, truth, and ultimately, eternal life..."

He continued to stare into space with his eyes fixated on the little square of tile. As he envisioned himself speaking, he saw the young men on the street listened attentively. Slowly, his words began to trail off.

This is too much to process in the middle of the night, he thought. He dragged his tired body back to bed and pulled the blankets over his head as he turned on his side. As he lay there, waiting to drift back to sleep, the thought suddenly occurred to him. That could be me in a couple of years talking to the young men in the neighborhood. In an instant, he questioned his thoughts. There's no way I can accomplish that, he thought. It's not like anyone in my family has ever gone to college. Too many of my family members haven't even graduated from high school or done anything positive with their lives. What makes me different from them?

The Spirit of God nudged him. The scripture from his Sunday school lesson the week prior entered his mind. "...With God, all things are possible..." His mind tossed back an answer.

If all things are possible with God, why are my family and my people poor, suffering and hopeless?

And then it happened. It was almost as if someone was standing right there in the room. The voice was clear, crisp and plain. *"For that very reason, I am calling you to minister to my people."*

Gilman quickly sat up in his bed, gripping the blankets with both hands as he anxiously scanned the room, looking for the person who spoke those words. Startled by the notion, he sat there in disbelief. "Me!? Minister? Yeah right." He said aloud. "What could I possibly do to help anyone, when I can barely help myself?"

Slowly, he leaned back until his head hit the pillow. Yeah right. Me. Imagine that. His mind twirled hundreds of thoughts as he attempted to get back to sleep.

~Two~

Gilman Everett, III. He hated his name most of his life. It was stupid to have a last name for a first name, not to mention the stupidity of being named after a father who wasn't ever around. His mother raised him alone, along with his older brother and two sisters. He and his sisters had the same father but his brother had a different father. Both were missing in action.

Shirley Rae Johnson, Gilman's mother, was a hard working woman, holding down three minimum wage jobs at one point. Those were days foregone. Her health only permitted the one job at the supermarket, but Shirley was not shaken by her circumstances. Her faith was strong and grounded in the Word of God and fellowship with other believers. She started attending Joshua Harvest Church when Gilman was 10 years old. Every week, she woke Gilman and his younger sister Candace, early enough for Sunday school. Occasionally, she was able to convince the other two kids to attend, but they were older and already on the course of teenage rebellion.

Gilman woke up to the smell of bacon sizzling and coffee brewing. The tunes of Yolanda Adams rang throughout the tiny house, -- "In the still of the moment, my voice can be heard, so listen carefully..." It was one of his mother's favorite CDs. He must have unintentionally listened to it a thousand times. He rubbed his eyes and tried to move his stiff body to get up. The events of the night replayed in his mind. The next track played, "Only believe, all things are possible..."

He forced himself out of bed, knowing that he had a busy day ahead. With his high school graduation now behind him, it was time for him to be the man of the house and find a good job. He was determined not to be like his brother.

He slowly walked into the kitchen.

"Good morning, son."

"Good morning." He leaned down and gave his mother a kiss on the cheek.

"How did you sleep last night?" She looked at him with a knowing glance.

8

"Well, it's funny you ask. I woke up with an upset stomach and there was something else."

"Oh yeah? Like what?"

Gilman told his mother about the daydream he had and the voice he heard in the doorway. She stopped what she was doing and gave him her undivided attention.

"Well, son, you should really pray about all of that. Remember the sermon in church a couple of weeks ago; the one about God being faithful and just to confirm what he calls you to do. My experience with God is that He will always respond to your request when you ask sincerely. I have found that waiting on God and asking for confirmation is the best thing to do when you're unsure."

"Mom, I wasn't exactly telling you that to say I think God is leading me to do *anything*. You asked me how my night went and I told you. That's all."

She slowly turned to tend to the bacon and grits. "Okay son." She knew not to press certain issues with him. She realized his stubbornness might cause him to miss the point totally. She just prayed a silent prayer, like she had done many times. "Lord, grant him Your wisdom, knowledge, truth, understanding, discernment, prudence and discretion. Order his steps, teach him Your ways, show him Your purpose for his life…" She prayed for the next hour.

~

As Gilman quickly walked down the street to the bus stop, he looked around at the single story brick houses. They were plain with faded shutters and small concrete steps. Many of the houses were boarded up. Cans, paper and other litter were scattered about the ground instead of grass. His heart wrenched with pain and embarrassment.

Graffiti symbols of the ruling west side gang covered the red of the brick, leaving Gilman with a nauseous feeling in the pit of his stomach. He despised the state of his neighborhood, knowing that the west side gang took great pride in the territorial signs of their crimes. The gang had been terrorizing the neighborhood for years, as their riffs with the east side crew left innocent victims of crossfire. Day or night, young or old, none were exempt. The violence had risen to unparalleled levels and Gilman loathed that fact.

Gilman walked dazed, staring at the brazen young man who boldly sprayed the wall as he occasionally stepped back, admiring his work. Gilman struggled to divert his attention to his job interview.

He was dressed in a pair of khaki pants, a button-down shirt, a tie and loafers. He knew how to dress the part from attending the largest high school in Delaware. He played basketball and was required to dress appropriately on game day. He also knew how to hook up his clothes from attending church on Sundays. He couldn't afford the suits worn by some of his friends. He didn't have very many slacks and dress shirts either, but he kept them clean, well pressed and neat. He walked with pep in his stride, full of faith that he would return with a job.

He boarded the bus, paid the fare and took a seat near the middle of the bus. It was crowded for that time of day. He sat next to the window, gazing out, with nothing particular on his mind. At the next stop, an older gentleman slowly made his way up the steps. With his cane in one hand, the man paid his fare with the other hand, being careful to balance himself. He slowly made his way toward an empty seat. Although the bus driver was kind enough to wait for the man to get halfway down the aisle, when the bus began to move, the man suddenly lost his balance. His cane toppled onto one of the seats and then the floor. In desperation, he gripped the back of the seat with one hand, barely holding himself up.

Gilman sprung into action as he jumped up and threw his arms around the man's torso to hold him up, using bended knees and one foot in front of the other as support. The man slowly pulled himself up with Gilman's help, still gripping the back of the seat.

"Th-th-thank you, young man," he stuttered, clearly shaken by his near fall.

"You're welcome. Sit here, sir," Gilman responded as he guided the man to the nearest seat. Gilman sat next to the old man and glanced at him. "Are you okay?"

"Yes. God bless you." He paused for a moment as his breathing slowly became steady.

"Thank God you were close enough to help me."

They sat in silence for a few more moments. Gilman stared straight ahead, deep in thought.

"What's your name, young man?"

"Gilman. Gilman Everett."

"I like that name. It's unique." He paused for a moment as if he were pondering some great matter. "God must have a unique calling on your life. I believe you will help many people, just the way you helped me today."

Gilman smiled, beaming respect and gratitude. "Thank you."

Could this be the confirmation that mom was talking about? Gilman questioned. She's said plenty of times that there are no coincidences in life. What are the chances that I would be in a position to help someone like this and they would say something like that? Naaa, he thought. Couldn't be, could it, God? He prayed silently. God, who am I that I could minister for You? If it is truly Your will, please send more confirmation. I need to hear Your voice clearly.

Gilman diverted his thoughts to his job interview, once again. He had rehearsed it a thousand times in his head, but he wanted to go over it just once more. He learned interviewing techniques from one of his business teachers at school who had taken an interest in him. His thoughts were filled with rehearsed answers to hypothetical questions. I want to work for your company because I have a lot of respect for the services you provide and you stand out among your competitors. The subjects I liked most in school are…

He approached his destination after walking several blocks from the bus stop. Optimistically, he announced his arrival to the receptionist at the desk.

"Have a seat. Mr. Johnson will be with you in a moment."

"Thank you." He rubbed his hands together, hoping that no one would notice that they were moist and shaking. He not only wanted this job, he really needed it.

As he sat down, his eyes were drawn to the local section of the newspaper on the mahogany side table. He couldn't believe his eyes. The headline read: *Riverside Shooting.* The pain in his heart gave him a sudden headache as he read the article blaming the west side gang for the shooting. His spirit overflowed with compassion and grief for the family of the young man who he had seen around the neighborhood on many occasions. The overwhelming feelings were mixed with indignation toward the article's accuser of the crime: the west side gang.

"Mr. Everett?" The man was standing in the corridor, arm extended, waiting to shake hands. Gilman took a couple of seconds to get himself together and quickly sized the man up as he shuffled to his feet. He was an older white gentleman, with salt and pepper hair, wearing a nicely tailored blue suit with a crisp white shirt and stylish tie.

"Yes, I'm Gilman Everett," he said as he shook the man's hand.

Looking directly into Gilman's eyes, the man began to speak. "Mr. Everett, I regret to inform you that, unfortunately, after your interview was arranged, there was a massive hiring freeze. We will keep your application on file and call you when the freeze lifts."

Gilman stared blankly at the man, clearly stunned. Just like that? I never even made it out of the lobby, he thought.

"Ohh...Okay." Gilman couldn't manage to utter another word. His disappointment was obvious. He looked at the receptionist who quickly looked down, pretending to be busy.

"I'm sorry, Mr. Everett. Have a nice day," he said extending his hand towards Gilman's for a departing handshake.

I'm sorry *and* have a nice day in the same sentence? Whatever, he thought.

"Thank you," he said as his head dropped. He walked through the revolving doors with his shoulders hunched low and his head hanging even lower.

As he emerged onto the busy street, his eyes were drawn to the clouds hovering in the sky. They were dark, full and ominous, completely hiding the sun. He hadn't noticed the clouds before that moment.

Great, he thought. Now I'm going to get caught in the rain too? Could the day get any worse?

His feet dragged along the sidewalk as he walked with his hands in his pockets, feeling completely dejected. I might as well put in a few more applications before I go home, since I'm already out, he thought. Let's see, where else would I want to work? He scanned the block for options. Oh well, I guess I can't afford to be choosy at this point.

~Three~

The bus ride home seemed to last forever. All sorts of thoughts rushed through his mind. Would he be stuck right where he was, like so many other brothers he knew? What options were realistic for him?

The barrage of thoughts made him think of his cousin, Calvin and how he ended up. Calvin was nineteen years old when he went to jail. Gilman looked up to Calvin because he was three years his senior so they had been close for most of Gilman's life. It had been too long since they'd been in contact. Gilman wondered how he was doing. He decided to stop wondering and find out.

~

Gilman sat at the kitchen table, meticulously mapping out his trip to Philly. Several bus and train schedules were scattered about the table. He figured he would need to take the train and two buses to get to CFCF, the correctional facility where his cousin had lived for the past three years.

"Going somewhere?" His mother asked as she walked into the kitchen with bags of groceries in both hands.

Gilman quickly stood to relieve his mother from her load. "Yeah. I've been thinking about Calvin lately. I'm going to Philly to see him." He placed the bags on the counter, unpacking the packets of ramen noodles first.

"I'm sure he'll be glad to see you. How was your interview?"

Gilman placed the hot dogs in the freezer as his demeanor suddenly changed. "Not very good, hiring freeze." He looked at his mother pathetically. "You know I really wanted that job, mom. I need something that will allow me to move up. I thought that job would be good for that. I don't want to flip burgers, wash cars or stand on the street corners to make a living, like so many other cats I know. And the service ain't no place for this black man. Those recruiters almost had me at one point, but thank God I rethought that. Besides, I need to stay close to home to help out."

"Seek God, son. I'm sure He will direct you to the path He has for you."

When the phone rang, neither one of them moved to get it since Candace managed to answer it after the first ring, no matter where she was in the house.

"Gil, the phone is for you," Candace's voice rang throughout the small house. He got up from the kitchen table and grabbed the phone on the wall.

It's probably Micah, he thought. I haven't spoken with her in a couple of days. She's probably mad at me by now.

They had been dating since the beginning of their senior year. They had been friends for months, talking on the phone for hours and walking each other to class. She was five feet tall, with honey brown skinned and shoulder length hair that she never kept in the same hairstyle. As an only child, her mother kept her dressed in the latest fashions. Gilman stood six feet, two inches tall, and had a handsome dark-skinned complexion with a tapered cut. They had been so into each other that they didn't associate with many people. That helped them manage to keep out of the gossip circles that were rampant in the huge school of over 2000 students. Fellow students had given them the label of "cute couple".

Gilman got on the phone and prepared himself for his girlfriend's tongue lashing.

"Hello?"

"Hey, man...," the voice trailed off into a somber whimper.

Gilman recognized the voice, though barely audible. "Marvin? What's the matter?"

"It's... Shawn..." Brief pauses and sniffles interrupted each word.

"He's been stabbed... in the chest."

"*What*? Where is he? How is he? How did it happen?"

"We're at Wilmington Hospital. Everybody's here. Micah's here too, man."

"Tell me. How is he?"

"They don't know. He's in surgery right now, but it doesn't look good." His friend's voice was muffled with sobs. "Gil...they say it's the west side."

Those words creep onto his shoulders and sat there like weights. "I'm on my way."

Gilman tried to keep calm, but the thought of losing his best friend was unbearable. Tears rolled down his face without a corresponding sound. He took a moment to pray. He had talked to Shawn many times about God but wasn't sure if he had truly accepted Jesus as his Lord and Savior.

Gilman entered the hospital waiting room to a dismal scene. Bellowing shrieks filled the hallway slapping Gilman in the face, spirit and soul. He didn't want to fathom the reason for the loud weeping. Tears streamed down the face of Shawn's father as he embraced his wife while she cried uncontrollably. Marvin was right. Everyone close to Shawn from the neighborhood was there.

When Micah saw Gilman, she jumped up and ran to him, almost knocking him over with the force of her embrace. She was wailing.

"He didn't make it, Gil. He's gone," she managed to get out through hyperventilating gasps.

The words seared through his ears and melted into his brain but he still refused to accept the horror of what he heard. The words just sat there, unable to penetrate the realm of his understanding. He couldn't understand. Numbness took over his body, starting from his head, slowly grasping his neck, his chest and his torso and finally worked its way down to his toes. Devastation haunted him; stood in his face and teased him. He wanted to shake his head and wake up from the nightmare. Tears fell from his face, but he couldn't feel them. He hugged Micah and comforted her with the little strength he had left in him.

~

Shawn's funeral was more painful than when he had been told about his untimely death. The initial shock wore off after a couple of days, but the funeral ushered the painful feelings back from where they were temporarily buried.

The church was packed with everyone from the neighborhood and more. Weeping filled the temple and sorrow crowded the building like thick low fog. Not a soul in Shawn's family maintained composure. The ushers worked overtime fanning, providing tissues and making sure that no one was about to faint. Gilman's weak frame could hardly hold Micah, who couldn't stop crying; no one could.

His best friend sobbed through the reading of the lyrics of Shawn's favorite song, moving the crowd to near exhaustion. His sister was brave through her rendition of, *His Eyes Are On the Sparrow*, until the end. It was just too much for her and everyone else to bear.

Through tear filled eyes, Gilman caught a glimpse of his brother several pews over. He blinked several times, trying to focus his vision. He had never seen his brother shed a tear and couldn't remember the last time he had seen Darrell in church.

22

Darrell sat there, dabbing his eyes with tissues, unaware that his brother looked on. Seeing his brother in mourning for the first time gave Gilman the sudden strength to get through the remainder of the melancholy day.

~

Gilman was already home from the funeral when Shirley got there. She had been praying heavily for Gilman since she found out about Shawn's death. She added fasting to her petition on his day of mourning.

Shirley slowly turned the doorknob to his bedroom and peeked in. She was a little surprised that he was asleep. She watched him briefly as he lay on his bed face down. She slowly closed the door and retreated to her bedroom. "Lord, comfort my son. Your Word says that blessed are those that mourn. Bless and keep him. Direct his path, oh Lord, and keep him in Your ways." She prayed in the solitude of her room for what seemed like an hour.

~Four~

Gilman called first to confirm visiting hours and planned his trip perfectly. The much needed journey to see Calvin symbolized his quest to find direction in his own life.

He walked with a steady and deliberate gait. He was contemplative about his plans for his future, which were slowly revealing their eggshell frailties. The reality of his world was not hunting for the perfect job that would catapult him into a wonderful career and save his family from the only neighborhood he had ever lived in. Depression had a chokehold and he couldn't see through the cloudy, murky fog.

Since his interview fiasco, he hadn't heard from any of the other job prospects, despite leaving countless messages. He was determined not to end up like his brother and father. He wouldn't be another statistic.

The tall metal gates reinforced those words in his mind. He thought back to when he saw his cousin caged up for the first time. He had to be strong while in Calvin's presence, but the moment he was alone, he instantly broke down. He hated prisons. He remembered the feeling of claustrophobia that engulfed him the last time he visited, and just couldn't imagine being confined.

Gilman walked through the gates and approached the guard booth. After displaying his identification and waiting a few minutes, he walked toward the visitor's entrance. The series of buildings were made of thick, gray concrete with barbed wire at the top. Maximum security style. He entered the building and approached the line to the sign-in desk.

This part wasn't fun either. The room was filled with mostly African-Americans and Hispanics, the former in larger numbers. Women and children sat wearing looks of boredom on their face while waiting to see the absent head of their households. Mothers who lost hope of seeing their sons at home waited to see them with care packages. This was no more than another grim reminder of Gilman's plight and that of his people.

The desk was high and several guards sat behind it, threatening, with their presence to keep the peace at whatever the cost. He signed in, showed identification and attested that he brought nothing to the person he was visiting.

He knew Calvin would be glad to see him. It had been a while. Not too many people from the family went to see him on a regular basis, since he was locked up in Philly. He would have had more visitors if he was in Gander Hill, the prison that was within walking distance from their neighborhood.

"Gilman Everett," the voice shouted out as if he were an inmate and it was time to leave the cell for supper.

He knew the drill. It was time for the purpose of his long journey. He raised a hand to the guard as he quickly stood. He thought of Shawn as he walked back to the visiting room. The joy floating within, from the anticipation of seeing Calvin quickly sunk underneath the surface as dark emotions struggled to gain control. Depression surfaced and tapped him on his shoulder, threatening to come back and play.

Gilman shook off the feelings and sat down in front of the glass, waiting for Calvin to come from behind the steel door. He knew he would make the best of his thirty minutes with his cousin.

Calvin appeared handcuffed and dressed in an orange jumpsuit, looking years older than when he first went to jail. The feelings of gloom could no longer ward off the burst of happiness that crowded Gilman's soul when he saw Calvin. Gilman's face lit up with a huge smile, matching Calvin's expression. They wished they could embrace one another, knowing that wouldn't happen for a number of years. Gilman reached for the phone.

"What's up man? You look better than I expected, I see you been pounding some iron in here," Gilman blurted out.

"Thanks, bro, just making sure I keep these fools off me. How's the fam back at River?"

"Mom's good. She's at the one job now, with her diabetes and high blood pressure and…you know, being overweight and all, the other jobs were just too much for her."

"Aunt Shirl gots to slow down. Yo, she worked mad crazy when we wuz kids."

"Ya know? Doing what she had to do. Now I need to be the one taking care of her unlike Darrell, who still don't got no job. I think he's shacking up with his woman nowadays. Man, I ain't trying to go out like that at twenty-four."

"Don't, man, don't. Stick with the plan, take care of the fam the legit way. I'm learning that the hard way. What's up wit Candace and Janice?"

"Candace is cool. The baby's just turned one. I'm trying to get her to at least get her GED before she hits twenty-one.

Janice just moved back in with the kids. She had to get away from that nut before I ended up in here with you." They shared a hearty laugh. "She's working, though; at John's kitchen, you know, up the way."

"So it's basically a full house in the three bed room, huh." Gilman shook his head.

"Whacha gonna do? I'm just trying to take care of business and get moms out of this situation once and for all."

Gilman glanced down momentarily, as a solemn gaze took over his expression.

"Did you hear about Shawn?"

"Naw, man what about Shawn…Jenkins, right?"

"Yeah, man…he's gone. It happened a couple of weeks ago; stabbed in the chest. West side's taking credit for it."

"Whaaat? They're still trippin', huh? Dag…I can't believe little Shawn is gone." He paused for a second to examine Gilman's face.

"And how's my little cuz doing now, for real, for real?"

"I'm kinda messed up by this one. Ya know Shawn was my ace. Me, him and Marvin were inseparable growing up. Seems like I'm the only one that stayed clear."

"Well, it's not like Shawn or Marvin had anybody to steer them in the right direction."

"Yeah, you name it, his brothers went to jail for it," Gilman responded. "West side in the blood. I knew something was up when Shawn started cutting school and stuff. It was a miracle that he even graduated with us. "

"Did Marvin graduate?"

"Man, Marvin should have graduated a *year* before us. Remember, he did time and didn't do anything else when he finally got back to school."

"Yeah, that's right. I heard that somewhere."

"He did finally graduate with us. You know we were kicking it at graduation." Gilman's eyes flooded with tears as he momentarily looked away.

"It's never easy. I'm sick of losing people to this place or the grave. Everybody walks around like this is what's supposed to happen. This is crazy, man."

"I know man. I'm really grateful right about now. You know I rolled worse than Shawn, hanging with dad's fam in Philly and hustling in the streets. I would have been better off hanging with you in River or in my neighborhood with cats like Brian who did something with his life. And thanks man, for looking out for a brother. It didn't register at the time, but I do remember everything you did and said to try to get a brother out of a situation."

Gilman cracked a smile. "I prayed constantly. You know mom was praying, too."

"I know, and prayer must work. I've been doing a lot of thinking in here, man. All the stuff about God and salvation that you and Aunt Shirley used to talk to me about is sinking in. Well...you know I've had lots of time to think and pray."

Gilman's face exploded with happiness. His body filled with excitement, dismissing the depression like determined rays of sunshine breaking through the clouds.

"I even have a Bible in here and I read every day. I need to turn over a new leaf when I get out of here. Ya know?"

"Yeah, man. I know. Mom will be praising the Lord when I tell her about this. I know I am. I've been doing a lot of praying and reading myself. You know, having my own personal relationship with God."

"I'm not surprised. I've never told you this, but, I could see you preaching somewhere on the street corner..."

He continued to talk, but Gilman stopped listening for a moment. Those words sat midair and stared Gilman right in the face. He couldn't believe his ears and couldn't help but to wonder if this was additional confirmation from God.

"Gilman...Hey man--"

"Sorry, man. When you said you could see me preaching…well, I think that God is calling me to do that very thing…in Riverside."

They both just looked at each other as they were simultaneously struck by the same epiphany.

"Pray about that, man, that's all. Can you believe those words are actually coming out of my mouth?"

They shared another laugh. "I've been praying about it. I just need to know the details, that's all. And I need to know it's right."

They continued to bring each other up to speed on the particulars of their lives. Gilman vowed to visit more often and to pray for his cousin on a regular basis.

~

The trip home was much shorter than the one to the prison. The visit with Calvin therapeutically soothed his aching heart for Shawn. It made him feel good that Calvin was alright and the news of Calvin's salvation warmed his soul. By the grace of God, he felt the dark could of depression and sorrow lift. The two words of confirmation and the vision he had on that night several weeks prior dominated his thoughts. The possibility of ministering for God didn't seem so far fetched anymore.

31

~Five~

Gilman still didn't have any interviews set up, but it didn't matter. Perseverance was taking hold, hand in hand with new and stronger determination. He was just glad to be himself again. He had mourned for Shawn for weeks and didn't get much else accomplished.

He planned a day of job hunting and quality time with Micah, feeling optimistic about the day and his future. Calvin's salvation had proven the power of prayer.

~

Micah sat on the couch, with the remote in her hand, flipping through channels but not really focused on the screen. A part of her was secretly grateful for a hiatus from Gilman since she had some things to take care of herself, but at that point, she was anxious to see him.

Should I tell him? She thought. How am I going to tell him? How's he going to react? A tornado of thoughts swirled in her head. She anxiously fiddled with the pillow on the sofa, staring motionless at the television screen.

Riinngg. Her thoughts were interrupted by the doorbell. She jumped up and peered out the peephole. Joy consumed her face.

"Hey you," she said as she hugged him.

"Hey, I missed my baby." He gave her a long passionate kiss on the lips.

They sat in the living room for half of the afternoon talking about his visit to see Calvin, Shawn's death and the funeral, his futile search for a job and the details of her life. They laughed and ate as they talked and occasionally watched television.

"Gilman...there's something I need to tell you." He questioned her with his stare.

"What is it?"

"Are you sure you won't be mad at me?"

"Uh...well, it depends on what it is. Are you cheating on me?"

"No, it's nothing like that."

Her pause made him look at her intensely.

"Gil, I'm pregnant."

"Pr—pregnant?"

She gently touched his knee. "Pregnant." Her tongue stuck to the roof of her mouth as she waited anxiously for him to say something.

"You mean to tell me I'm going to be a father? I don't know what to say, Micah." Guilt flooded Gilman's heart ushered by tormenting insecurities. Gilman thought about the vision he had and whether he could actually carry out something like that.

I have sinned and come short of God's glory. Who will listen to me? How could I be the one chosen to minister to anyone?

His words reflected his uncertainty. "A--are we ready for this?"

"Do we have a choice at this point?"

He didn't answer the question. "Well…how do you feel about this?"

She sat up as she bit her fingernails. "My reaction was just like yours. I was in total disbelief. You should have been here when I told my mom. She had a fit. She seems to be getting used to the idea now, though. This has made me think about doing something with my life, like maybe enrolling in school or something."

He gave her a long, endearing stare as he leaned over and kissed her softly on her head. Compassion momentarily chased away the guilt as he slowly began to accept the words she uttered. "You've given this a lot of thought, haven't you?"

"I've known for a couple of days now. I needed to accept it first before I could tell you. Besides, you were really going through, so I just couldn't put that on you right then."

"You're sweet, but you shouldn't have carried that load alone." He paused as the shock continued to settle in.

"I hope I get some calls soon about a job. I must have filled out a dozen applications today," he said with a frustrated tone.

"Something will come through. I'm going to start looking for a job soon, too," she responded.

They sat silently for a few minutes as thoughts flooded his mind. He chose his words carefully. "I know we've discussed this before but, I need to really focus on God and perhaps...stop...you know...doing what we did to get us in this situation."

"You mean sex, right? Just be direct with it." He nodded his head in response.

35

She couldn't accept his words any more than he could initially accept hers. The conversation he referred to was one sided. Despite all of Gilman's efforts, she had not accepted Jesus as her Savior so she didn't share his guilt.

They sat, uncomfortably in silence for a few minutes. He couldn't believe she clammed up and really couldn't process anything else.

"If you don't mind, I'm going to head home and get some rest." He gave her the kiss that he knew she needed and leaned over to squeeze her tightly.

"Are you okay?" She lifted his chin with her fingers and looked into his eyes.

"Yeah, I'm okay. What about you?"

"Yeah, I guess I am."

Their departing embrace was so long that it seemed to last forever. Neither one of them wanted to let go.

He held in the anxiety mixed with fear, bottled like a volcano about to erupt, until he got home.   It took about that long for the shock to partially wear off and for him to grasp the fact that he was going to be a father. He went into his room, pounced on the bed and released the feelings inside. Free flowing tears poured out the contents of his soul.

Shirley heard Gilman come in an hour earlier and knew something was bothering him. She listened intently outside of his door and finally knocked.

"Come on in mom," Gilman decided he needed his mother at that moment.

"What's the matter, baby?" She asked as she took a seat next to Gilman on the bed. She slowly rubbed his back.

"Mom, Micah just told me that…she told me that she's…well, you're going to be a grandmother again." He steadied his breathing as he spoke, but the tears continued to flow.

Although Shirley was surprised and somewhat disappointed that another one of her children hadn't followed her teachings of abstinence, she knew it was not the time to come down too hard on him. Gilman had been through a lot and needed her support and acceptance.

"Baby, I know you have mixed emotions right now. But you and Micah have to move on from here. Sweetheart, you know God designed sex for two devoted people in a marriage, but you have to live and learn. I love you, son. Trust in God at this time and always. You know, you've been through a lot in the past month or so. Seek God and learn the lessons He has for you in these trials. You know the Bible says, count it all joy when you are tested and tried. Remember that dream you had not too long ago, think of how that fits into your life right now. God works all things together for good for those who love Him and are called according to His purpose."

"I know, mom, and you were right about confirmation." Gilman wiped his face with the back of his hand.

"God has confirmed the message He gave me through Calvin and a total stranger. I just feel so unfit to do anything for Him right now."

"Do you want to pray?"

He sniffled his answer, "Yeah."

As Gilman sat up in his bed, he felt comforted by his mother's words of wisdom. She gave him a long hug and held his hands as she prayed.

"Heavenly Father, we acknowledge You in everything we do, in the good times and in the bad. Forgive us our sins because we have all sinned and come short of Your glory. We need Your awesome mercy and grace. We ask that You lead us not into temptation and deliver us from the hands of the evil one. We thank You for all that You have provided us with, a roof over our heads, food in our mouths, clothes on our backs and every good thing that comes from you, Lord.

We lift up Gilman and Micah unto You today, Father. Prepare their minds and hearts for parenthood. Give them an understanding of Your will for their lives. Guide them and direct them in Your ways of righteousness, Lord. Give them Your wisdom, knowledge, truth and understanding to be able to give this child what it needs, spiritually, mentally and physically. We give You all of the glory and honor and praise, Jehovah-Jireh, our provider. We pray these things and all things in your Son's name, the Messiah, Jesus. Hallelujah."

As they embraced again, the last remnants of fear and anxiety slithered out of the room, expelled by the love of God.

"Thank you, mom. I love you."

"I love you too, baby. Rest in the Lord, Gilman, rest in the Lord. He will direct your path. Just trust Him."

She kissed him on the forehead and left the room. She continued to pray and he fell into a peaceful slumber.

~Six~

It had been two weeks since he got the news from Micah and nothing had surfaced on the job scene. Determined not to be expelled for long, stress hovered in his presence, threatening to creep into the muscles of his flesh. He knew he needed to pray and exercise to ward off the assault. With much tenacity, he continued to complete application after application.

During one of his job searching excursions, he had noticed an advertisement for a local college, featuring a degree in theology. The thought that he had to consider other options for his future weighed heavily on his mind. Life suddenly increased the stakes and just finding any old job didn't seem appealing to him anymore. Through adversity, he could see the path more clearly.

His body stirred as his ears sent signals to his brain to turn off the alarm clock. It was Sunday morning and he wouldn't dare miss an opportunity to be fed at that point in his life. He turned off the alarm and rubbed his eyes as he sat up in bed. He could hear his niece running around in the other room. She was always the first one in the house to awaken, rousing the unsound sleepers. He could hear bits and pieces of the conversation between his mother and Candace about going to church. It was always the same. Candace protested and his mother insisted and pleaded. He knew his mother would never give up.

He got down on his knees and prayed earnestly. "Thank you, God, for your great mercy and grace in allowing me to see another day. I praise Your name, God, for Your name is holy and deserving of all praise, honor and glory. I ask Your mercy upon me, for I have sinned and come short of your glory. Guide me and direct my path in this and every day." He continued to pray for his mother, his siblings, Micah, his purpose and future and the neighborhood.

When he rose to find the outfit he would wear to church, the spirit stirred within, causing him to fall back down on his knees. As he just sat there with is face in his hands and his elbow propped up on his legs, he heard a voice.

"The people perish for lack of knowledge. Take plain spray paint and cover over the idolatrous graffiti that symbolizes the state of mind of the people. Do not be afraid of the drug dealers and menaces who put it there. This is the beginning of your street ministry in the city of Wilmington."

Gilman hesitantly responded, "God if this is really what you want me to do, please confirm it."

Gilman jumped slightly at the sound of the phone ringing. Who could be calling at this hour?

"Hello?"

"Hi."

He loved the soft, sweet sound of her voice.

"I know it's early in the morning, Gil, but I just want you to know that I love you and I miss you. I know you've been busy and that's why we haven't talked in a couple of days. I...I understand that you've been through a lot and I just want you to know that I'm here for you. You've been under a lot of pressure lately. I know that you and your mom have been praying for me, cause... I accepted Jesus as my Lord and Savior last night at the revival."

"God is so good," he excitedly interrupted. "Thank you, Father. I've been waiting so long to hear those words."

"I know, Gil. I really believe that He has a purpose for my life now and I know he has a purpose for your life, too. Whatever God is telling you to do, Gil, just do it. Do it with boldness and God's strength. I'll be praying for you."

He marveled at the words of wisdom coming from Micah.

"I'm going back to church with my grandmother this morning and I'm looking forward to going to church with you soon, so...umm...I have to go. Maybe I'll see you later on?"

"Are you kidding me? Right after church. Micah..."

"Yeah?"

"I love you, too. Words can't really express the way I feel right now. God *is* good. Thank you for being obedient to God in calling me. It means more to me than you could ever imagine."

They hung up and Gilman fell down on his knees and worshiped God. "Thank you Lord, thank you for Micah's salvation. Praise your holy name. I really believe that you used Micah as the vehicle for Your confirmation. Have mercy on me. Please, God, forgive me for asking, but please send more confirmation. I will be a willing servant, just, please confirm Your will."

~

Shirley and Gilman listened intently as Reverend Jacobs delivered the message. "...Elijah was a man of God, called according to a purpose. What was that purpose and how did he carry it out? Turn with me, if you will, to the book of first Kings, chapter eighteen, verse sixteen." Reverend Jacobs read the verses.

"Now let me put this in context for you. The reigning king at that time was Ahab and first Kings, chapter sixteen, verse thirty-three says that 'he did more to provoke the Lord' than all the kings of Israel. And to make matters worse, he was married to Jezebel, the great idolatress and persecutor of God's chosen people. Now imagine this, many of the prophets of God had been put to death by Jezebel and then God tells Elijah to present himself to the very people who are persecuting prophets. It took a great deal of faith for Elijah to present himself to Ahab. Let's continue to read."

With passion and conviction of spirit, Reverend Jacobs read the passage detailing how Elijah revealed the idolatry of the false god Baal and his prophets by challenging them to make an altar to their god Baal and prove his power by calling to him to bring down fire onto the altar.

Reverend Jacobs highlighted Elijah's humanity in taunting the prophets of Baal when they pleaded and prayed and nothing happened. He continued to read the passage.

"...And Elijah told the people to saturate the altar that he built to Jehovah, the one and only living God, not once, not twice, but three times." His voice went up two octaves with each soaking of the altar.

"Why do you think that Elijah went to such lengths?" He paused for congregation consideration as he searched the faces in the pews. "The purpose was for God to prove that He is the one and only living God. And fire came down from heaven and not only burned the sacrifice, but licked up every drop of water that fell down from the altar.

Elijah's purpose was to speak the words that God told him to speak and to be a vessel to carry out God's will. Isn't that a common purpose for us all? Aren't we, as God's people, supposed to do the very will of God out of obedience? Although we all have different gifts, some to prophesy, some distinguishing among spirits, some the message of wisdom, and so on, are we not called to a purpose?

If and when God speaks to our hearts, as He did with Elijah, we must obey His command..."

45

Tears flowed down Gilman's face as he sat with his arms extended in praise. Shirley graciously thanked God for sending him another word of confirmation and was grateful that she was there to witness it. They were in awe over God's display of mercy and grace and his faithful patience in giving him the confirmation he needed.

Gilman's thoughts were focused and deliberate. He knew that was a sign from the God. He spoke in a whisper. "Lord I accept the purpose to which You call me. Be with me and direct my path."

~Seven~

With much thoughtfulness, Gilman planned the commission that God gave him. He would do it in the wee hours of the morning so that no one would see him. There was an hour when even the drug dealers went to sleep. He went to the local hardware store and carefully selected a color very close to the color of the brick that the houses were made of. Restoration, he thought. I have faith that God will restore the minds and physical state of my people.

He spoke to himself out loud. "And first thing on Monday morning, I will begin to do whatever I need to do to get enrolled in school."

The night was cool and still, not a soul seemingly stirred about. He had set his alarm clock for 3:45 a.m. and went to bed in his clothes. As soon as the alarm clock started to buzz, he quickly turned it off and rose with ease, as if he had gotten a full night's sleep. He stealthily moved about the house, so as not to awaken anyone, grabbing the bag filled with fifteen cans of spray paint.

He worked skillfully and quickly, spraying paint over the graffiti. It was not possible to do every house in the entire neighborhood, but he was able to cover the symbols of the west side gang on all of the houses near him. He prayed as he worked and felt a tremendous sense of peace in accomplishing the will of God in the task.

~

"Who did this?!" He shouted, spewing profanity as he ranted and raved. It was immediately noticeable and none of them were happy about it. They took it as an immediate threat and insult, especially since it was done in such a covert manner.

"Find out if this was done by the east side!" He barked.

~

By that evening, they knew it was Gilman. They snatched up homeless Harry, as they called him, who squealed in their grip. He had been gleefully watching in approval as Gilman did as God instructed.

The knock on the door wasn't what Shirley was accustomed to. She lived in the neighborhood for years. She

48

didn't start any trouble and didn't get any trouble. The beating on the door was menacing. She prayed as she approached the door.

She stopped at the living room window and cautiously pulled back the curtain. There were three young men standing at the door. She had seen them hanging around the neighborhood before, doing nothing worth while. She cracked the door just enough for them to see her face.

"What can I do for you young men today?"

"We're looking for your son."

"And what business do you have with him?"

The spokesperson looked at his comrades as they looked at him. They weren't prepared to answer questions, just to ask them.

"Well...we wanted to discuss something with him. It won't take long."

"I can relay the message."

The spokesperson was irritated and in excitement, blurted out, "He disrespected us and we gonna get wit him."

"What do you mean?" She inquired indignantly.

"We put the graffiti there because this is our territory. He disrespected the fam by painting over it."

49

She understood what they meant, but she was just a little puzzled. She thought she was aware of all of the comings and goings of her house and couldn't believe that Gilman hadn't shared this with her prior to doing it. She boldly spoke up on Gilman's behalf.

"Gilman is my son and he's God fearing. I don't know what you young men were taught, believe or live by, but my son lives by the convictions that God gives him. You all need Jesus. If you contend with Gilman, you contend with God. He is called to minister according to the will of God and His purpose. He's not some opposing, rival gang. He lives here, just like you live here and if what he's done makes our community a better place to live, you should be happy. He's not a stranger to you. You know him and grew up with him. This is not a personal vendetta that he has against you. The love of God has stirred him to *help* you. Take heed."

They stood there somewhat taken with her words, but refused to budge.

"Why are ya'll standing there looking at me like that? Don't you know that I practically raised all of you?" She focused in on the spokesperson. "I knew your grandmother before she passed away. She would be so disappointed in you. She used to take your little tail to church every Sunday, God bless her heart. And now look at you." She peered at them sternly.

Just then, the unexpected happened. Her words convicted their souls. She didn't realize that God was using her to plant a seed that he would grow later. They immediately felt ashamed. Shirley had a way of demanding respect from the most disrespectful of persons, especially in her neighborhood.

Their reproach was evident by their expressions. Shame flooded their faces. The purpose for which they came suddenly seemed futile. They had to admit the truth in what she was saying. Gilman a threat? That *was* absurd. They only saw him toting a Bible, going to and from school and walking in the neighborhood, mostly dressed like a geek. He certainly wasn't making a move on their turf.

Apologies flew from their mouths, one by one, as they excused themselves off the porch with their heads down.

Shirley softly exhaled a sigh of relief and closed the door. "Thank you, Jesus. God, Your mercy and grace endures forever." She continued to pray.

Gilman was sound asleep, oblivious to his mother's intervention.

*

~Eight~

He really didn't know where to start or what to do. It wasn't as if he knew someone who had gone through the process of applying to college. He decided to start with familiar territory, his high school. He called his old football coach, who led him to his old guidance counselor. He discovered that he needed his transcript, an application and recommendations to begin the process. His counselor also told him that he would most likely be able to waive the admission fees.

"Don't put your eggs in one basket, Gilman. Apply to more than one school." His counselor's words resonated in his mind, over and over but he felt something in his gut about one school. He applied to three local colleges and hoped for one.

Imagine that, he thought, Gilman Everett hoping for college admission. Thank you, God for Your grace and mercy. I can't believe that I'm the first person in my family to even attempt to get into college.

His faith was colossal, looming larger than he could have ever imagined. There was no conceivable way, in Gilman's mind, that he wouldn't get into one of those schools.

~

As the weeks transpired, Gilman read his Bible daily and amazingly, he began to read other books that he wouldn't have thought of reading: *The Invisible Man*, by Ralph Ellison, *The Song of Solomon*, by Toni Morrison, *Their Eyes Were Watching God*, by Zora Neale Hurston and the most difficult, yet liberating, *The Reckoning*, by Randall Robinson. Invariably, he needed a dictionary to remotely understand some of the books. He had discovered the African-American section of Walden books at the Christiana Mall.

His brain yearned for more. From the moment it started its slow rusty churn, the oil of desire sprinkled curiosity until it became an insatiable thirst for more. Knowledge was in his grasp. He needed to know. He needed to find the answers. He felt they existed somewhere, out there, maybe in the smallest corner of the world tucked under a rock in Cameroon, Africa, or under the majestic untouched snow-topped mountain of New Zealand. Maybe both had two different pieces of the puzzle.

God brought him to a wonderland of wisdom and knowledge that his counterparts couldn't ever fathom in their lifetime of mental and physical enslavement.

Lord, have mercy on them, he thought. Have mercy on my community and the communities like mine. They perish for lack of knowledge.

~

He had been checking the mail for over a week. This time would be different. He had the letter in his hand and suddenly, he felt queasy and breathless. The anticipation of getting the long awaited answer and the anxiety over the possibility of not getting in struck him in the chest like a hurling unexpected punch.

He ripped open the envelope and read the first sentence. We are pleased...

He knew what those words meant. He scanned to the bottom of the letter for confirmation. "That's what's up! Mom! Mom! Mom!"

He ran around the house with so much excitement that it startled everyone in the house.

"Mom! You won't believe this! Mom!"

He waived the letter wildly in the air. His sister looked at him like he was crazy and his nieces and nephew ran around the house with him, not knowing what they were running for.

He ran up to his mother and lifted her two feet off the ground. He twirled her around and slowly lowered her back onto the floor. He hugged her tightly and kissed her on the cheek.

"Mother," he said as he calmed his voice, "Your son, Gilman Everett, the third will be attending college and studying in the field of theology."

Shirley stared at him in amazement. She couldn't believe she was hearing those words. Her love and gratitude to God overwhelmed her. She hugged him tightly.

"Thank you, God, for Your mercy and grace upon my family." She took his face in her hands, and brought her face two inches from his, as she looked him straight in the eyes. "I'm so very proud of you son. God has called you to a great purpose. Continue to seek Him and He will direct your path."

They embraced as his sister watched in astonishment. Tears rolled down Candace's face. She knew this was a miracle; *her* brother going to college. She immediately felt a sense of hope for her life. She approached her mother and brother and included herself in the hug. Shirley and Gilman prayed silently.

The door knob jiggled and everyone turned their heads to

see who was coming in the house. Darrell's face appeared in the doorway. They were all surprised to see him. Other than at the funeral, they hadn't seen, nor heard from him in over a month and assumed that he was staying with his girlfriend. He struggled to get the big black duffle bag that he was carrying through the door. He looked puzzled at the sight of the group hug.

"What's going on in here?" He asked bothered by the fact that he wasn't feeling as good as everyone else.

"Well...your brother just gave us some great news. Tell him, Gilman."

Gilman spoke proudly, "I got accepted to college. *I'm* actually going to college."

Darrell looked down as his feet and glanced at Candace, then at Gilman.

"That's wonderful," he managed to blurt out in a strained voice. "The first person in the family to go to college. Mom must be very proud," he said sarcastically.

"God is so good. This is an answer to my prayers." She paused, questioning Darrell with her gaze. "And what have you been up to? Are you staying *here* now?"

Darrell indignantly dropped the bag on the floor, as his facial expression changed from embarrassment to anger.

"Why are you harassing *me*? What, I can't stay here now? Get off my back!" He spit profanity and saliva at the same time.

"Hold up, wait a minute, Darrell." Gilman had witnessed Darrell's disrespectful actions towards his mother once too many times. He wasn't going to allow Darrell to ruin this moment for her.

"What, you the man now? Whacha gonna do?

Darrell charged across the room and stood in Gilman's face.

"You're not coming in here disrespecting our mother like that, you good for not--"

"Who you calling a good for nothing..."

Darrell pushed Gilman so hard that he fell several feet back onto the floor, hitting the chair on his way down. But he didn't stay there for long. Gilman quickly rose to his feet and released a four-part combination on the face of his eldest sibling.

Darrell was caught off guard. Gilman never challenged him before that moment. He was momentarily stunned and just stood there, taking the punches.

She had enough; enough of the fight and enough of Darrell. He had come and gone, without a moment's notice, taking advantage of her and disrespecting her for too long. She had been praying for her son and praying for patience. She would continue to pray, but he had to go.

Her calmness amazed everyone in the room. With soundness of conviction, she walked up to her sons, separated them and stood in the middle, facing Darrell with her back to Gilman.

"Son, you're going to have to leave. You're a grown man and it's time for you to make it on your own. I can't do it anymore. You weren't raised to disrespect me like this and I've been very patient up to now. You know I love you and I will always pray for you, but you must leave, *now*."

She didn't raise her voice, but he would have felt better if she had. That moment was filled with firsts for him. Although he had seen this same conviction in his mother, he never heard her utter words like those. He knew he had come to the end of the road.

Both of them were still breathing heavily with clothes disheveled. Candace was no longer in the room. She grabbed the kids and took them in the bedroom. She could foresee what was about to happen and didn't want them to witness anything. Gilman stood his ground behind his mother as Darrell shamefully picked up his bag and headed for the door. He walked out without looking back and without saying a word.

Shirley couldn't hold it in any longer. She burst out tears of sorrow for her son. She knew he didn't know where he was going. Gilman consoled his mother with a long hug, as her body jerked from sobbing. He hadn't seen her cry often, and didn't like it when he did. He hated the fact that he had to go there with his brother. A sense of remorse overcame him, accompanied by compassion.

"Sorry mom."

"No need to be sorry son." The tears continued to flow as she sniffled while she spoke, "I could see this coming for quite some time. I was dreading this moment. Your brother needs a lot of prayer. That's all we can do for him right now."

"Let's do that now. I'll pray." He gently took his mother's hands into his. "Heavenly father, we come before you right now, first asking for forgiveness for our sins. We lift Darrell up in prayer right now…"

The entire focus of his prayer was his brother. When he was finished, Shirley felt a warm sense of peace. She was grateful to God for the breakthrough in Gilman's life and would stand in intercession and faith for Darrell. She knew she wasn't alone. There would be two prayer warriors praying for Darrell regularly.

~

The drama of the day didn't keep him from falling asleep like a baby, that's why he couldn't understand why he was wide awake all of a sudden. He didn't move for a couple of minutes, as he tried to get back to sleep. He looked over at the clock. Three o'clock in the morning. Then it dawned on him.

I was up at this time before. That's strange, maybe I should pray, he thought.

Gilman got down on his knees and prayed, worshipping God and thanking him for His mercy and grace. Then it occurred to him to just kneel there, in silence and wait upon the Lord.

The voice was as soft as a gentle breeze in the summertime, and more faint than a whisper. *"You will speak to the masses. Though I send you, remember that the battle is mine. You will fight against the drugs and ignorance that ruin a people. Don't be afraid. I will be with you."*

A tingling sensation flowed throughout Gilman's body and his eyes filled with tears. The realization that the voice of God actually spoke to him made his spirit glow with overwhelming joy. He remained on his knees and worshipped God.

"Guide me, Father and lead me in the way that I should go."

60

The sun shined brightly through the curtains as Gilman rubbed his eyes. That wasn't a dream, he thought, God *is* actually calling me to do something. He was overjoyed with enthusiasm; ready to take on the world.

It was such a beautiful day that he wanted to go right out into the neighborhood and do what God told him to do. He thought about what he would say and remembered back to that first night. It amazed him that he still remembered. "That's it. That's exactly what I'll say," he boldly declared.

He hurriedly got dressed and purposely put on a white t-shirt and jeans, so that he would fit in and not turn them off with his appearance. He left the house without praying, feeling very capable of handling the situation.

Several people already occupied the corner not too far from his house. His heart raced a hundred miles per hour and his mouth was as dry as an Arizona afternoon in mid-summer. He carried his Bible and the words that he heard himself speak months prior. He was full of pride and self-confidence.

"What's up, ya'll." He managed to say with a pint-sized amount of courage.

With humor on their faces and curiosity on their minds, they sized him up. "What you doin' out here, straight man Gil?" One of them jeered.

61

Anyone could see that the one who spoke was the leader of the corner. He stood six feet, two inches tall, donned Allen Iverson inspired braids, as did many of his counterparts and weighed approximately 240 pounds. Big Mike. Everyone knew who he was.

"Just wanted to discuss a matter with ya'll."

They looked down at his Bible as he spoke. Big Mike laughed hysterically.

"About what? Not that Bible stuff." He laughed again. "Man, get the heck outta here wit that crap. West side got business to handle out here."

One of the other guys on the corner lit what looked like a cigar but reeked of marijuana. A young girl approached the guys, from what seemed like, out of no where.

"Can I get a dime bag?" She asked as she pulled the crumpled up money from her back pocket.

Big Mike looked at one of the guys and the guy reached into the pocket on the inside of his jacket and pulled out a sandwich bag filled with, what looked like, to Gilman, oregano. They made the exchange right there in broad daylight.

"Yo, man, I told you to get outta here." This time Big Mike used curse words to express his impatience.

"Do you feel good about yourselves? Do you care about your life or the lives of anyone else? Come on, tell me, do you feel good inside, or empty? You don't even realize how you're playing out the master's plan."

Gilman was interrupted by sudden yelling. "Yo, yo, five-o!"

The young men began to scatter like ants; everyone but Gilman. He was standing there puzzled, watching the backs of the three guys who were standing there, as they ran in different directions.

Then he understood. All he could see was flashing lights. There before him were two dark blue cars with yellow writing. State Police. Their guns were drawn and they were charging directly at him.

"Hold it right there. Don't move."

His legs were shaking uncontrollably. The Bible fell from his hand as his arms flew up in the air. He bent down to pick it up.

"I said hold it right there!"

He remained bent down, as he remembered the many instances in the media of how black men were beaten and killed because of making a wrong move. No doubt the actual numbers were even greater.

The others stopped in their tracks also, having only managed to get thirty feet or so from the corner.

Gilman started to pray out loud. "Jehovah, God of Abraham, Isaac and Jacob, you are my redeemer and my salvation; my fortress and very help in my time of need. Hear my plea."

The officer forcefully spun Gilman around as he barked obscenities at him.

"What did I do? I didn't do anything. I was standing here talk--"

"Shut up. You have the right to remain silent, everything you say can and will be used against you. So shut up. You have the right to an attorney, if you cannot afford..."

Gilman's words trailed off as he prayed silently. He watched two other officers handcuff two of the other guys who had stopped in their tracks. Everyone except Big Mike was taken away. He was the only one standing there who wasn't wearing a white t-shirt.

Gilman rode in the back of the police car with the guy who was smoking the blunt. The blunt had been thrown the second the warning left the other guy's mouth. Gilman frantically looked around. Until that moment, he never would have imagined that perspective. Less than three feet from his face were protective bars. The guy sat next to him gazing out the window as if it was business as usual. They both wore handcuffs and no seat belt. The chatter of the police radio muttered non-stop jargon of who-dune-it and where they could be found information.

This has to be unreal, Gilman thought. This has to be a nightmare.

"...yeah, that's right. We got three that fit the description of that liquor store robbery."

He looked at the guy next to him with a look of indignation.

I can't believe this. This guy doesn't look nothing like me or the other guy, Gilman thought. Is he color blind?

The guy next to him was several shades lighter, with extremely different facial features, not to mention, several feet taller. Gilman continued to size him up. He looked down at his own attire, realizing that they were all wearing the same thing; white t-shirts and jeans. Then it dawned on him. That was the problem. They all look the same, just like inmates walking around with no sense of real identity; not even understanding what they do.

And I'm no better, he thought. I've been duped, too. How did we get to this point?

He turned to look directly at the guy sitting next to him.

"How did we get to this point?" Gilman repeated the question out loud.

"What?"

"How did we, as brothers, get to this point? Look at us. We're being shipped off in shackles and chains; the innocent and the innocent of this crime, at least. We're in the same boat by sheer virtue of the color of our skin and shirts. Can't you see? Open your eyes, man. There's only one way to freedom, the Messiah, Jesus. God sent His one and only Son as a sacrifice for our sins. You don't have to stay where you are."

He was actually listening. He had no where to go and no where to hide. No one had ever talked to him like that. All he knew was the life he was living. His mother was strung out on the very thing he sold, so he made his own way. He didn't care or think twice about the life he was living. It was Russian roulette.

"You're playing into the hands of those who feed off your labor, man. Just like picking cotton. You get pennies of what they get, at much less risk for them. There's no way out except the bars, which are shackles, and the grave. And your mindset, man, you're enslaved in the mind. All you know is getting the money, smoking the weed and getting more money. You're killing each other slowly and every now and then, quickly. Bang. Another black man out of the way. Can't you see? You have a purpose for your life that you're missing out on. God is waiting for you to repent and seek Him. There's a world of knowledge, hope and opportunity out there for you, brother."

"Shut up, back there! Shut up."

He looked at Gilman with a hopeless desperation.

"Think about it, man," Gilman whispered. "We'll talk more later. Okay?"

He slowly shook his head. "Yeah, that would be okay."

"What's your name?"

"Rodney."

"I'm Gilman."

Thank you Lord. Gilman prayed silently. He prayed for Rodney, Big Mike and the others in his neighborhood. His faith was miraculously intact. At first, he didn't fully understand why he found himself in this situation, but at that moment, things were clearer. God was using him in the midst of the horrible situation.

The rest of the ordeal was demeaning, at the very least. They were man-handled, pushed, shoved and treated like cattle waiting to be branded. And branded they were; fingerprinted, photographed and numbered. He was humiliated and mortified.

He didn't know what to expect next. They were shuffled off to another room and ordered to remove their clothing. It was time to be searched.

"You have this all wrong," Gilman desperately tried to plead his way out, "I was just standing there---"

"Sure you were, be quiet!"

The other guy knew what was coming next. He felt sorry for Gilman.

"Look, he really was just standing there; with a Bible in his hand at that. He's a goody-goody, church going, school boy. And that was his first time out--"

"I said shut up. Get those clothes off. You know the routine."

Gilman was debased and demeaned beyond grief. He had heard of body cavity searches but never imagined anything like that.

He found himself in a five by five holding cell. He was alone and grateful for that fact. The cell was filthy, with a small bench and a similarly dirty toilet.

Why would anyone want to do anything that would come down to this, time and time again, or even risk this? He continued to pray as the hours slowly passed.

"Gilman Everett, come on out." The bars opened. Thank you God, Gilman thought.

"Someone is here for you and you've been cleared. You're free to go."

"Free to go?" He said with an air of righteous indignation. "I should have been free from the word go. You didn't care about whether or not I was innocent when you pushed and shoved; when you shackled me with those pieces of metal; when you raped me of my dignity. I had a Bible in my hand, and nothing more. "

"Just save it and get out of here. You're all the same, anyway, eventually."

The words pierced him a thousand times like tiny arrows. His suspicions about some innocent black men in the justice system were validated and crystallized but an overwhelming peace came upon him, instead of anger. For the battle is not mine, it's Yours, God. Have mercy on him, Father, for he knows not what he says or does, Gilman prayed earnestly. He thanked God for the miracle of patience and forgiveness in his life.

~Nine~

Gilman sat alone in his room, deep in thought of the past, present and future. The thoughts streamed, words teamed through his consciousness: life.

Deep within the walls of my inner consciousness, no longer echoes of mindless chatter, painting strokes of dilemmas with no real answers. What do I think? Previously, of no words my mind drank, my soul sank, slowly into the muck of my meager existence. I longed to be free. Me, somewhere in this space with no place for the "me" of the world. Who is my ally, my mentor, the invisible foe? My foe permeated the air I breathed, saturated the food I ate and stalked my very last breath. Should I lay to die in the wilderness of the ghetto, never knowing the assailant from the UPS man seen in my neck of the woods once every two years. That tunnel, I couldn't see my way out. Where was my first step.

It didn't seem to be beneath me. The ground slips out like my brother's prank of grabbing the shag rug the moment my desperate foot takes hold.

I couldn't get up. I couldn't see out of the hole. My anger ensnared me further into the trap. The noose tightened, unbeknownst to me. What do I know? What image can I grasp? Television betrays me with images of nothing that can set my soul free. Promises of dreams; my reality roars with stitches and tears from such harsh laughter.

Who is Cash Money, Colin Powell or Jesse? What about Reverend Sharpton? That's it. Reverend Sharpton. I remember the autobiography on television. He had obstacles. How do they relate to mine? Am I walled in by the hood? What should I do? I need a plan; can't make my mind understand.

Why us? How did we get here? Why are we stuck here? My brain is yielding desire for ponderous activity. I can't commit ghetto career choice suicide. I can't commit the crime of ghetto murder one, felony of the first degree to the city where I'm from. The city wails and cries sadness of a slow suicide/homicide. The culprit hides in the shadow breathing vapors of greed, lust, supremacy, pride, arrogance and hatred into the air we breath. But we're left holding the smoking gun. This ain't no fun. I wanna be free. What are my alternatives; my

71

choices? How can I get life to release it's choke hold? My mind is slowly working. My brain thrives. This is good. I can begin to live.

I've been aimlessly wandering through life; not thinking, knowing or growing. Dead man walking. So many just like me. Useless brain matter; the birth of my foe's desire. I was gripped up, sucked up, pent up, bound link by link; the chain around my brain. My foe held the key. Safe in the hole in the wall nestled behind a painting, hoarded and passed from generation to generation on the walls holding up 6,000 square feet of blood stained ghosts, still runnin' the show. So where do I go to get the key? How can I see…in the dark? The mirror is pitch like the night, just like me and that ain't right, echoes a jovial society.

All jokes aside. The race started hundreds of years ago and I'm laps behind. How do I stand a chance? How do I get in the grind?

Jehovah, you are my salvation. You fight the foe. You run the show, so… I must go, obey and follow the way.

~

As horrible as his experience was, Gilman was thankful that all things worked together for good. The experience of being falsely accused and arrested would forever be embedded in his mind as first-hand knowledge of the subject of his calling.

His life would never be the same. He read his Bible even more, knowing that God was preparing him for that vision he saw months ago.

Rodney had become a very close friend and faithful Bible study partner. He started going to a reading tutor and enrolled in a GED course. Gilman finished his first semester of college with a 3.8 GPA. They spent hours at the library and Kingswood Community Center, which was just blocks from where they lived.

Micah was due to give birth to what the ultra sound indicated, was a boy. Gilman was thrilled and couldn't believe that he was actually thinking of making the baby the fourth Gilman Everett. Micah found a job and decided to put school off until after she had the baby. Gilman's success motivated her to keep her goals alive.

The thought occurred to Gilman that maybe the support group that he formed for young men should evangelize with him. Perhaps fifteen or twenty young men, Gilman thought. He was on his knees, praying about the idea when he heard the voice in a small whisper.

"Take only one, so that no one will be able to boast that it was his doing."

Gilman understood perfectly. There was one lesson that

he had learned by then. He needed less confirmation. He was learning to trust in God.

"Gillllllman. Telephone."

He thanked God for the answer, praised him for just being God and ran for the phone.

"Hello?"

"Gilman Everett?"

"Yes?"

"This is Stephanie Carter, MBNA hiring chair. You put in an application several months ago, but there was a hiring freeze. Would you still be interested in the job?"

Gilman was knocked off of his feet. "Yes," he said with enthusiasm. He made arrangements to interview for the job.

~

"I got it! Mom, I got it!" He ran to his mother's room.

"Yes, Gilman. What is it? What's all the commotion?"

He lifted her off the ground and spun her around.

"I got a job, mom. Eleven dollars an hour and the long awaited help that you need."

"Praise God! Praise God!" She responded with excitement matching his.

"And you won't believe it mom, guess who I ran into today, working as a janitor at Kingswood?"

"Who?"

"Darrell."

Her eyes suddenly filled with tears. "Did you--"

"We talked for a few minutes. He's hanging in there, living with his girl, but working and trying to get on his own. Give him some time, he'll be here for a visit, I'm sure. And yes, we made up with an embrace. I didn't tell you that I saw him at Shawn's funeral. Mom, he's actually attending that church now."

They praised God together, rejoicing in His goodness.

~Ten~

A job, college and plans to move kept Gilman busier than ever before. He was grateful, though. He gave his mother money from every paycheck to help with the bills and to save so that the family could move. He also saved for the baby and the proposal he so eagerly planned. He was starting his second semester in college and growing stronger in the Lord. He and Rodney regularly walked the neighborhood and spoke to the young men on the corners. Many of them listened and attended the Bible study sessions at the community center.

Gilman's support group met once a week at the center. He prepared lessons on what it means to be a responsible man, understanding the background on the plight of the African-American community and what it would take to move from ignorance to the knowledge of the truth and education, along with many other topics. He acted as role model and mentor to many young men and became respected in the neighborhood.

Many listened to his words of wisdom. "...we are the minority in this country. How is it that the minorities can comprise eighty percent of the prison population? Now let's talk about the prison, money making industry itself. Would it surprise you to know the number of prisons in this country have almost doubled in the last twenty years, while the laws for non-violent drug users have become even stiffer? The sentences for possession alone are disproportionate for blacks and that's one of the main reasons that we comprise the majority of prison population.

Now think of your neighborhood. There's no coincidence. It was designed and built to be a war zone. You don't bring the drugs in. You just go to jail or kill each other for passing it off to the rest of your community, as it slowly dies. How long are you going to allow this system to assault you, your friends and your families? You don't have to stay ignorant. You can be free. Jesus died so that you can be free. The Bible says, 'My people perish for lack of knowledge.' God sent me to tell the truth; to give you the real deal. No holds bar. I've given you the facts and statistics, not so that you can be angry and frustrated. That was the life you lived before when, deep down inside you knew something was wrong, unfair and unjust. But now that you know, what are you going to do about it? 'Seek ye first the kingdom of God and His righteousness and all these things will be added unto you.' You must repent of the life you've lived at the hand of the unseen foe."

Tears rippled down the faces of many of the young men. The spirit of the Lord had begun to penetrate the broken-hearted. The young men began to open up and discuss the pain of not knowing their fathers or having to witness the struggle of their mothers. They spoke of the frustration of not understanding what was going on in school, for years. Some of them had been passed along, unable to read. They talked about how the only life they knew was watching their older brothers or older guys in the neighborhood hustling. That was the only life that they thought they could live. The so called "American dream" was an American fantasyland for them. They lived in America war zone, where democracy was a joke. They didn't rule anything: not even the hustle on the street. They needed to talk and they did that every week. The healing had begun.

~

Gilman spent a great deal of time at the community center, talking to the young men who came to the sessions. New people attended regularly, but he knew the time had come for him to tackle the streets with stronger fervor. He prayed and fasted for weeks and felt it was time.

He thought back to the first time he hit the streets. He had learned so much since then and grew leaps and bounds. He thought of how God had used that experience in so many ways to help him to grow and to establish lasting friendships.

He put on his cream turtleneck sweater, a pair of jeans and his black boots. He hadn't worn a white t-shirt since that awful day. He grabbed his black leather jacket and his Bible and walked out of the house. Rodney said he would meet him on the corner.

He immediately spotted him. It was like he was reliving the experience. There he stood; Big Mike with several others, just standing there. He hadn't seen him in a while. He had spent months in jail for selling. Gilman stopped in his tracks as his mind flashed back to the last time he saw Big Mike. Frosty air puttered its way out of his mouth as he struggled to steady his breathing. "Give me strength, Father. Give me your strength and power. Let Your Holy Spirit speak as the words from my mouth."

"Do not be afraid, for I am with you."

He continued to walk towards the corner. With every step, he felt strengthened and rejuvenated. His confidence did not rest with his abilities, but with the faith of the confirmation that God had given him time and time again; it was grounded in the experiences of faith, through trials and tribulation that God allowed over the years. He had faith in the calling of God.

"What's up, guys?"

Big Mike quickly turned around with a look of familiarity on his face.

"I thought I recognized your voice. Not you again. Didn't you learn your lesson the last time?"

"I sure did. I learned many valuable lessons from that experience and I thank God for it. The question is, have you learned any lessons since the last time we saw one another?"

"Who the he--!"

"Look, man", Gilman boldly interrupted, "I'm not out here to start trouble. I know it sounded like I was getting smart, but I'm posing a real question to you. What are you doing out here man? How was the joint? Is that what you want for your life? Or would you rather end up in the morgue before your time? This doesn't have to be all you know."

"What are you talking about?"

"You don't have to stay where you are. You don't think because you've been taught not to think. This is what you've accepted. There's another existence out there waiting for you to discover and live. If you accept what you've been told, without reading and discovering for yourselves, how will you know?

Jesus came to set you free and only God can make you whole again. I was born here, just like you. No one in my family graduated from high school, let alone college. Yet I stand here before you with a semester of college under my belt only by the grace and mercy of God. You too can have freedom and salvation by accepting Jesus as your Lord and Savior. He came so that you may live and have life more abundantly, not killing each another and the community by being a vehicle for those who don't live here but are the real foes.

What's happening is genocide. Righteous, responsible black men are an endangered species. It's modern day slavery and more of us in the jails than anyone else. Open your eyes and see. Accept Jesus and be free. Come out of ignorance and believe that you can do all things through the Messiah. You were born into this place. This is all you know. For some of you, it was all your mothers knew. You breathed it and was bred it.

You didn't pick your parents or the color of your skin or the unjust laws or hierarchy system that you were born in. But Jesus loves you, the sinner and the poor. Somewhere, someone lays claim to breeding a new type of human, one that does not have a father and a mother. That would be you and me that was bred. Now be fed the truth of the gospel and be free from the lie of deceit. "

Just then, Rodney walked up and gave Gilman a masculine, brotherly hug.

"Roe? What's up, man?" Big Mike greeted Rodney with a pat on the back and their usual handshake, River style.

"You cool with this cat now?" Big Mike asked in disbelief.

"This cat *and* Jesus as my Lord and Savior. Man, just listen to him. He's coming with lots of love. *We* come with lots of love. I know where you are, man. Remember I was right there with you. The dead walking. Not caring about a soul, not even ours.

Man, that day me and Gil got arrested changed my life. He was innocent and we all knew it. But that's the society we live in and it's time for us, as black men to start looking at that system and to start to thrive in it instead of being chained in by it. We need to take care of our families, the legit way and step out of mental enslavement. I didn't want to go to the joint anymore. You know it's the truth man. Just think about it."

Rodney's familiar voice and words penetrated Mike's spirit. A sudden glow of warmth overshadowed the hard callous

82

covering his heart. He couldn't understand what he was feeling. Miraculously, Big Mike's eyes began to overflow with tears. Somehow, what they were saying made sense. It was as if blinders had been removed from his eyes; thick wax removed from his ears. The others watched in amazement. Gilman and Rodney embraced Mike.

"The Bible says that God so loved the world that He gave His only begotten Son as a sacrifice for your sins. Are you ready to accept Jesus as your Lord and Savior?"

Mike knew that was the answer. He really didn't enjoy that life, and he definitely didn't want to go back to prison. He believed what they said to him.

"Yes."

"All you have to do is say a simple prayer. Do you want to do that?"

"But I don't know how to pray. I've never prayed a day in my life." All shame was gone. He stood there wide open and vulnerable; waiting for the answers to questions that he didn't know he had until that moment.

"Just repeat after me. Father God..."

Mike repeated Gilman's words with deep sincerity.

"...I am a sinner and have come short of Your glory. I repent and turn away from my sins. Forgive me of my sins.

Thank you for sending your Son to die on the cross for me. I receive and accept Jesus into my heart as my Lord and Savior. Don't leave me or forsake me, Father. Be with me, guide me and direct me. Thank you, Father."

They stood there for a while, sharing their testimony with Big Mike and the others. Gilman spent the early part of the evening praying and thanking God for His grace and mercy in the salvation of Big Mike and the others.

~

As he lay there on his bed, reflecting on the day it slowly occurred to him. What happened that afternoon was exactly what he saw that night, almost a year prior, right down to the details! He was even wearing the same outfit.

What a glorious day that was for Gilman. He had experienced a lot as a servant of the Most High, but it was at that moment that the calling of God to His purpose was confirmed. Regardless of what life would bring, the trials and the tribulation, he knew his help came from God and that he should look to him to direct his path. Gilman danced before the Lord and worshipped God until he tired himself out.

Bonus: From, *My Little Book of Poetry: Marni Speaks, Marni Seeks Truth*

Innate Abilities

Innate abilities
To consider the possibilities
Innate abilities
To work through responsibilities
~
So
Spend the time
To think about
To read about
To pray about
To be about
To become about
The business
Of just who you be
~
Fly sister fly
Roll brother roll
Go sister go
Go where you need to go
To be
True to thyself
New to thyself
Curious to thyself
Beautiful to thyself
Handsome to thyself
Intelligent to thyself
Happy with thyself
~

Because of the choices that you make
Which are grounded in all of the truth
Of every action that you take
~
Spiritual creatures we are
Spiritual creatures we are
Spiritual creatures we are
~
To speak the truth
Act the truth
Be the truth
Consider the truth
At all times
Be about the business of the truth
At all times
~
If I can't
Speak the truth
Act the truth
Be about the truth
What would that make me
A Liar
~
The truth speaks for itself
The truth stands for itself
The truth is itself
The truth is whole
The truth is pure
The truth is absolute
~
Why must you lie to your brother
My sister
Why must we hate
On each other
My cousin
Why can't we get together
As family
Brother against brother

Daughter against mother
What is the answer to this conundrum
~
Ideas to proliferate
Substantiate
What you know innate
Go on educate
Take time to create
Get prostrate
To a state
Of awareness
Bareness
Wholeness
Fairness
Holiness
Clean up the mess
Satan can't touch the blessed
~
Innate abilities
To consider the possibilities
The responsibilities
Innate abilities
To work through the possibilities
The responsibilities
That we have my sister
We raised this nation
We should not have raised this nation
By ourselves
We raised our sons
We should not have raised our sons
By ourselves
~
We were stripped of
We were robbed of
We were raped of
We were taken of
Taken of
We were taken of

87

Our dignity
Of who we be
Black woman
~
Innate abilities
To consider the possibilities
The responsibilities
That you have my brother
Too many brothers out there
Without hope, without a prayer
Too many brothers locked up
Modern day slavery run amuck
Too many stuck
Shackled in mindless indoctrination
Not thinking, knowing, living, growing
Because
You were stripped of
You were taken of
You were beaten of
Degraded of
Your dignity of who you be
Black man
Ain't recovered from
Till our community
Is free
There aren't enough of us free from
Lack of dignity
~
Innate abilities to consider the possibilities
The responsibilities
Of what we need
What they need
What they need from us
What we need from them
Why should I sit back for another moment
Another moment
And close my eyes
Close my eyes

To all that I see
To all that I see
To all that I be
To all that I be
I've got to be me
I have got to be me
I've got to be what God called and created me to be
~
In His purpose
In His image
In His Will
In His Way
I must submit to the righteousness that I was called to
I must humble myself to the hand of the Almighty
In prostrate I must be
Stripping away every layer
Of emotional scars
Of battered abandonment
Rejection
From the very beginning
Healing has begun
~
Innate abilities
You have, my sista
To consider the possibilities
You must consider your possibilities
~
Innate abilities
You have my brother
To consider the responsibilities
You must consider your responsibilities
~

Mercy

Mercy, mercy me
Things ain't what they used to be, naw
Things ain't what they used to be see
We...We
Us, that's you and me
We have got to be different
We can't stay the same
We have got to enlighten
Every member of the game
In this game of life
There's too much strife
There's too much hurt
And too much hate
People just can't relate
Everyone's perceptions cloud the debate
Right and wrong
Wrong and right
Where is our fight
I say let there be light
Truth first starts the healing of the pain
For us He was slain
Ain't no time to be lame
It's time to reclaim
Rebirth and rename the game
I've got to proclaim
Through enlightenment
That's the only reason
Why I was sent
And rest no more
No lies to adorn
~
We have to teach the kids
All the reasons why
We have to teach the kids

Not to fall but to fly
They're killing each other
And incarcerated, following the lie
Mindlessly indoctrinated
Why, oh why
Could Willie Lynch be the reason
His ways still pleasin' ...His grave
His legacy still greasin'...Our minds
Think about it if you will
The process of thinking he did kill
As he set up for generation, after generation
For hundreds of years, still clear
We haven't recovered
Shackled in the mind
My people
Shackled in the mind
It's time for a revolution
See I think that revolution
Is the only solution
To this here pollution
Of the mind
Revolutionary methods
To un-wash the brain
Cleanse the stain
The revolution is the truth
Let us tell the truth
Let us speak the truth
Revolutionary methods
To rid us of pollution
Corruption
Destruction
Can't stop talking about it
Until our people, our children
Are thinking about it
About something
Thinking at all, thinking at all

Us up against the wall
Our hands and legs spread tall
Ya'll can't you see
The state of mind
Of the majority
Are the educated in the
African-American community
The majority
Are the enlightened in the
African-American community
The majority
Are the responsible men
In the African-American community
The majority
Is spirituality the majority
Of our youth
If you can't say yes
Then it's time to be set free

~

Oh mercy, mercy me
Things ain't what they used to be
The radio it rings
The sound
Of fornication bound
The sound
Of Sodom & Gomorrah bound
Explicit lyrics of lust, lust, lust
It's okay to sing about where to lick me
Where to stick me
In our society
The adults they let it be
Mercy, mercy me
For the children to see
It's okay says society
Right is wrong
Wrong is right

That's the song they sing
With all their might
Sober is wrong
DUI is right
That's the tune they chant
With all their might
Crystal to drink
That's all they think
In lap dances their minds sink   .
Adorned in nothing but a mink
Drink, Drink, Drink
Whore of Babylon does wink
Our society does sink into a pit
Of death it stinks
When will we
Stop to think, think, think
But that's what they said about Rock n' Roll
103.9 disc jockey tolls
At half past nine
That's his reply
To the sound of my words
Freedom of speech is what they say
Freedom to destroy morals of yesterday
This is what I say
Things ain't what they used to be
How far will we
How far will we
As a society
How far are we
Willing to go
How much are we
Willing to show
Slippery slope, this is a slippery slope
Every sense of right to blow
Act like we know
No righteousness we glow

I ain't willing to go
On the Sodom & Gomorrah show
Does anything go
Does anything go
Does a n y t h i n g go
Don't say no
Till you open your eyes
Look around at your world
Anything goes
On the radio
Practically anything goes
On reality shows
Anything goes
On the videos
Violence cries the video game woes
That's why our children don't grow
Anything goes
In the political game show
Steal the presidency is what we know
Contradictions
Truth derelictions
Responsibility in remission
It's all fiction
It's a lie
Mercy, mercy me
Things ain't what the seem to be, naw
If we don't take a stand
Grab the mic
Make a plan
This land
Will stand
In the shoes of S&G
Can't you see
That's the prophecy
Get yourself right
Is the only

Possibility
Of being
Free
For eternity
If things ain't what they used to be then
And things ain't what they used to be now
Then we need to be on the ground
Prostrate
Let's debate
What we create
What we delegate (to our youth)
Our present state
This realm's fate
How we relate...to the truth
Let's get it straight
Our way, our gait
Before it's too late

~

Mercy, mercy me

Study Questions

1. What did the gang symbolize from the story of Gideon in the Bible (Judges 6-8)?

2. What did the scene of Gilman hanging clothes in the first chapter represent from the story of Gideon in the Bible?

3. What are the references to idolatry in the story and how does it relate to the story of Gideon?

4. What did the removal of the graffiti symbolize in the story of Gideon in the Bible?

5. What are the ramifications of the recent Cash Money Millionaire inspired white t-shirt craze as it relates to African-American males?

6. Since the Isrealites were enslaved due to their disobedience and idolatry, how should we, as a people learn from this, since we were similarly enslaved? How do the many prophecies against Egypt in the Bible (Jeremiah 16, Ezekiel 29 and Isaiah 19 & 20) relate to the African-American community's plight and that of the African Diaspora?

7. Where do we, as African-American people go from here? What responsibility do we have to each other and what responsibility do we have to impact and change the prison statistics (starting with our treatment of little black boys in day care centers and the healing of the heads of our households, the African-American man)? Are we under a modern-day slavery of sorts, with our men in jail and mental enslavement?

8. Examine our community carefully. Have we fully recovered from slavery?

9. Decipher Gilman's introspection (pgs 78-80).

About the Author

Marni M. Williams is originally from Chester, Pennsylvania and currently resides in Middletown, Delaware with her husband and four children. She defied all odds as a teenage mother of two before graduating from high school when she graduated from Penn State University with a B.A. in Social and Behavioral Sciences. She later graduated from Temple School of Law with a Juris Doctor degree and practiced in the areas of corporate and commercial litigation, human resources, stock transactions and contracts. She did her final stint practicing law as a prosecutor in Philadelphia.

Following her passion to devote her life to working with teens, she's currently the Project Director of Communities In Schools, the largest drop-out prevention program in the nation at the largest high school in Delaware. She occasionally teaches as an adjunct instructor, teaching business law at Wilmington College.

In June of 2002, Marni self-published her first book, *My Little Book of Poetry: Marni Speaks, Marni Seeks Truth* as a one of a kind, limited edition collection and released the book in paperback in February, 2003. As one of the winners of the Power 99 Def Poetry Contest for her poem, *Idolatry*, she launched her spoken word debut on the air at Power 99 on July 7, 2002. Since then, she has performed as a spoken word artist at various venues including churches, poetry events, a comedy show, book signings, community events, colleges and radio stations, among others.

Keep your eyes on this powerful new voice on the literary scene. Marni's first novel, *Mere Presence*, is scheduled to be released in January, 2004. But look for her second book of poetry, *Uncovering the Truth: Poetry and Other Things*, to be released later this year. Additionally, Marni will release *Marni Speaks, Marni Seeks Truth: The CD* in July, 2003. On the CD, Marni performs favorite poems from the book with a background of sounds including a mix of jazz, blues and hip-hop.

Marni's fictional work includes a spiritual message immersed in real life drama. Often, she draws from her legal background to give readers a sense of true justice. By the grace and mercy of God, Marni has always set her goals high and had the faith to achieve them. She gives all glory to God for all of her accomplishments and believes that her life was designed by Him to be an inspiration to others. This is just the beginning of a blessed ministry of inspiration.

ORDER FORM

Please send me _____ copy (ies) at the cost of $12.00 per book with regular shipping (takes 2-3 weeks).

My total due is $_____
Ship Order To:

Name:_____

Address:_____

City:_____

State:_____

Zip:_____

Telephone (_____) _____

Make Checks or Money Orders Payable to:
Marni M. Williams

MAIL TO:
WILLIAMS ENTERPRISE PRODUCTIONS
P.O. Box 812
Middletown, Delaware 19709
(302) 376-4379
williamsenterpriseproductions@msn.com
marniwilliams.com

PRODUCING FROM THE DEPTH OF THE SPIRIT;
A CONCEPTUALIZATION OF CREATIVITY